Pyramid Chart

This chart shows categories of things arranged from smallest to biggest.

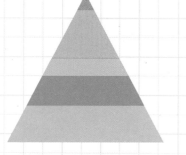

Map

This chart shows where things are.

Tree Chart

This chart shows where ideas, families, and things came from. It's very useful when showing a family's ancestry!

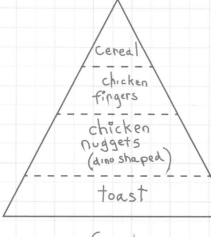

Cereal

chicken fingers

chicken nuggets (dino shaped)

toast

Uma's food pyramid

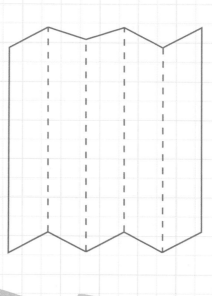

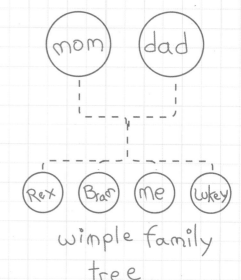

mom   dad

Rex   Bran   me   Lukey

wimple family tree

For

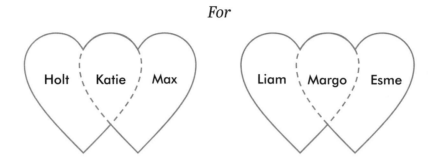

All rights reserved. Published in the United States by Anne Schwartz Books, an imprint of
Random House Children's Books, a division of Penguin Random House LLC, New York.
Anne Schwartz Books and the colophon are trademarks of Penguin Random House LLC.

Visit us on the Web! rhcbooks.com
Educators and librarians, for a variety of teaching tools, visit us at RHTeachersLibrarians.com

Library of Congress Cataloging-in-Publication Data
Names: Larsen, Reif, author. | Gibson, Ben, illustrator.
Title: Uma Wimple charts her house / by Reif Larsen and Ben Gibson.
Description: First edition. | New York: Anne Schwartz Books, [2021] | Audience: Ages 4–8. |
Audience: Grades K–1. | Summary: "A young chart maker faces a challenge when she is given
an assignment to make a chart of her own home"—Provided by publisher.
Identifiers: LCCN 2020027305 | ISBN 978-0-593-18118-8 (hardcover) |
ISBN 978-0-593-18119-5 (library binding) | ISBN 978-0-593-18120-1 (ebook)
Subjects: CYAC: Charts, diagrams, etc.—Fiction. | Dwellings—Fiction. | Home—Fiction.
Classification: LCC PZ7.1.L3714 Um 2021 | DDC [E]—dc23

The illustrations were rendered in mixed media and Adobe Illustrator.
Book design by Ben Gibson

MANUFACTURED IN CHINA
10 9 8 7 6 5 4 3 2 1   First Edition

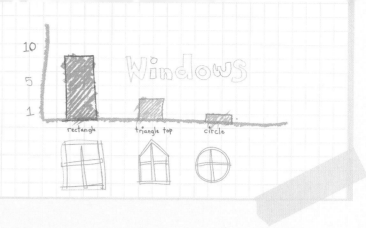

Uma Wimple
Charts
Her House

by Reif Larsen and Ben Gibson

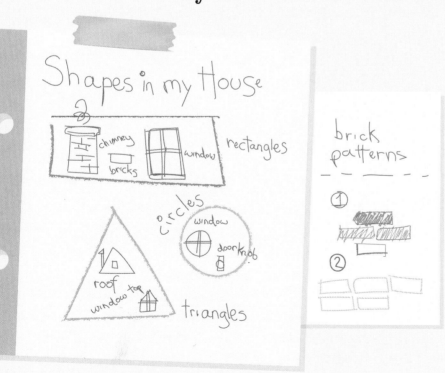

a·s·b

anne schwartz books

This is me, Uma. I make charts.

This is my best friend, Buster.

Buster tears my charts into tiny pieces.

I made my first chart when I was four.

Did you know that my dad is the only person in our family whose pointer finger is longer than his ring finger?

by uma age 4

mom

dad

sex dram uma lukoy

When I was five, I made a chart of all the trees I passed on the way to school.

my school

spruce

maple

maple

pine

my house

Did you know that maple trees make little helicopters called samaras to send their seeds far away from home?

A good chart should make you see the world in a new way.

Like this chart I made in the park.

Who Holds Hands?

almost always

pretty often

almost never

grown-ups hold hands with their kids

kids hold hands with kids

grown-ups hold hands with grown-ups

dogs don't have hands

Pegasus | Unicorn

Alicorn!

rainbow color order

1 2 3
4 5 6 7

After that, I started making **LOTS** of charts.

Wimple family daily screen time

recommended

Luke
Rex
bran
Uma
mom
Dad

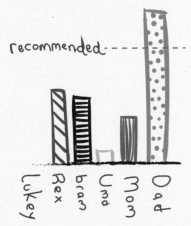

LOVe code-breaker chart

X | O
↓ | ↓
KiSS | hug

Wimple family screens

a)
(size comparison chart)

b)
c)

d)

a) tv   b) computer
c) tablet d) phone

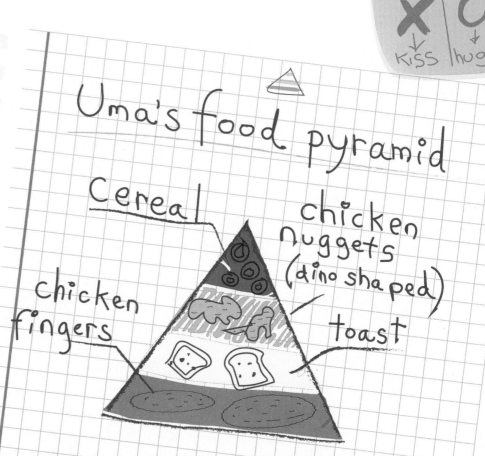

Uma's food pyramid

Cereal

chicken nuggets (dino shaped)

chicken fingers

toast

At school, my teacher calls my charts doodles.
They are not *doodles*. Come on, people!

Then one day a tiny miracle happens.

"And so, for our next project, we're making
a chart of our own home," says Mr. Easley.

"A what?" I say.
"A chart," he says.

Holy moly Gorgonzola!

My head begins to spin. . . .

Oh, the possibilities!

Oh, the pressure!

How can I chart something so big, so important, so complicated?!

On the way home, I'm in a panic.
I study each house for ideas.

You might be thinking:
"Just draw a chart of your home, Uma!
No big whoop."

Yeah, well . . .

. . . it's not so easy.

I mean, just look at my house. . . .

The windows!

The porch swing!

The pattern of the bricks!

I go up to my room and begin to draw.

I draw and draw.

Something is not quite right.

What makes my house . . . *housey*?

I decide to do a survey.

First stop, Dad.

"What makes a house housey?" I ask.

"I don't know," says Dad. "Maybe it's the smells?
Pancakes delivered to you in bed? A cup of hot
chocolate when you have the shivers?"

"Hmmm," I say,
and make some notes.

Next stop, Mom.

"What makes a house housey?" I ask.

"It's a feeling, isn't it?" says Mom. "Like when we went back to my old house,
it just felt so different without Grandpappy and Nanna there.
It wasn't the same at all."

"Hmmm," I say, and make some notes.

Third stop, Rex and Bram's
tree house.

"We're busy," says Rex.
"Just go."

"What makes a house housey?" I say.

"Making songs with the band," says Bram.
"Finding that perfect beat together."

Strange drum sounds start coming from his mouth.

"Hmmm," I say.

I'm not sure my survey
is working.

I press on to my last stop, Lukey.
Up the eleven steps to the attic.

Step three makes a sound like a donkey.
This is like ringing Lukey's doorbell.

"Uma!" says Lukey. "Buster!"

"I don't know what to do," I say.

"Come in," he says. Papa New Guinea, Lukey's iguana, blinks.

"Want to see my new butterfly?" Lukey says.
"It's a Hessel's hairsteak."

"Sure," I say.
But I have a hard
time holding on
to everything.

Lukey's magnifying glass crashes to the floor and breaks.

"Drat it all!"
I cry.

I crash to the floor
and break too.

Lukey kneels next to me.

"Don't worry," he says, and picks up the magnifying glass.
"It still works."

"I'll never finish my chart," I say. "It's impossible."

He gives me a hug.

"Nothing is impossible," he says.

At dinner I don't touch my food.

"What's the matter, Uma Looma?" says Mom.

"You don't like my Bolognese?" says Dad.

"She says 'no ways' to the Bolognese," Rex raps.

"I'm thinking," I say.

"Can't you eat and think?" says Mom.

"There is no think, only do," says Lukey.

So I do . . .

and do . . .

until finally . . .

I find my way home.

Pie Chart

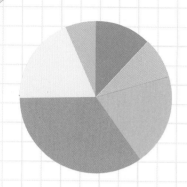

This chart shows how a whole is divided into parts.

Bar Chart

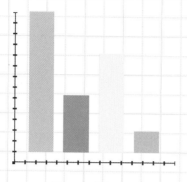

This chart lets you compare different categories of things with each other.

Venn Diagram

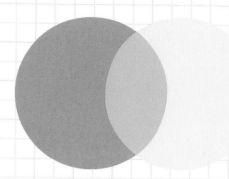

This chart uses overlapping circles to show what groups do and don't have in common.

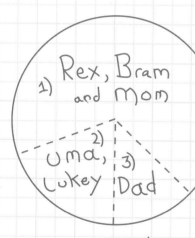

1) Rex, Bram and Mom
2) Uma, Lukey
3) Dad

pizza pie chart
(wimple family topping preferences)

1) cheese
2) pepperoni
3) pineapple (gross)

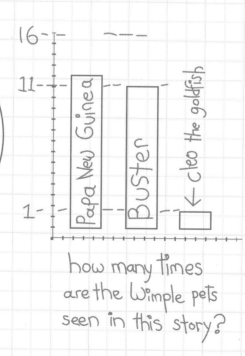

16 ―
11 ―
1 ―

Papa New Guinea

Buster

← cleo the goldfish

how many times are the Wimple pets seen in this story?

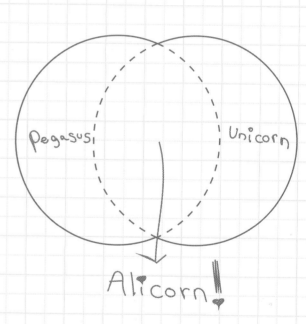

Pegasus

Unicorn

Alicorn!

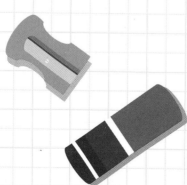